NORSE MYTHOLOGY

Tales of Norse Myth, Gods, Goddesses, Giants, Rituals & Viking Beliefs.

Kory Aumont

CONTENTS

INTRODUCTION

Before their conversion to Christianity, the Nordic populaces (also known as the Vikings) had their own rich and vibrant native belief system. The core of this native religion is now what we refer to as Norse Mythology. It is filled with stories and lore that allow us to peek in to the lives of the Vikings. Like Greek and Roman Mythology, Norse Mythology revolves around gods and goddesses with highly complex, yet fascinating characters such as Loki, Frigga, Thor, and Odin.

It is interesting to take note that the religion of the Nordic people never had a true name (ie Christians, Muslims, Jews ect). Those who practiced the religious rituals, that prayed to their favorite god or goddess would adhere to the ways of their ancestors. However, those who continued with their old practices after the introduction of Christianity to Scandinavia were referred to as "heathens" or people who lived on the heaths or wasteland and the stereotype became part of the Middle Ages.

Basically, the main purpose of religion is to connect with the divine, and the religion of the Vikings follows the same path. The Norse religion provided specific ways that were fitting for their traditions. Some aspects of Norse Mythology could be eccentric for us who are now living in the modern era.

To appreciate these stories, we need to have an open mind so we can truly understand the common quest to live a meaningful life. And while it has been thousands of years since the Viking warriors started their invasion, we are still inspired by their conquests and the divine beings that they invoke to seek guidance in fulfilling their destiny.

As we explore Norse Mythology, we will realize that these people lived in an enchanted world, and their religion was never to seek salvation from the suffering of this world, but rather they seek to connect with the divine so they can marvel at their creation. The Norse religion didn't make the universe appealing: the unfairness, strife, or sordidness of humanity, but rather acknowledged and praised the efforts to master the world of doing great deeds.

CHAPTER ONE

THE VIKINGS

In regards to the Vikings, people typically conjure images of barbaric warriors who enraptured hell to the shores of Europe in the Middle Ages. Historically this is true, as the Norsemen launched hundreds of attacks to plunder and raid the rich monasteries, castles, and towns. But beyond this brutish reputation, the Vikings had a rich and dynamic culture that still has its influence in our modern world to this very day.

The Vikings shaped the homeland of contemporary Denmark, Norway, and Sweden long before they became countries. These Nordic countries were mainly rural with no centralized settlements. Despite the common opinion that all Vikings were barbaric warriors, majority of the Norsemen were farmers or fishermen.

In fact, the etymology of the word Vikings came from the Scandinavian word *vikingr*, which is roughly translated as pirate. This word is basically used as reference to sea voyages and was primarily used by Scandinavians as a verb. Hence, *vikingr* means to go "viking" or seafaring. The function of the term is pretty much the same as to go "kayaking" or "skiing". Not all sea voyages were about raiding towns, as the trading of goods were a huge part of the Viking way of life.

It is also interesting to take note that the early accounts mentioning people from the Northlands were not called Vikings. The term only appeared in the 11th century. Rather, early records refer to them as Dani (Danes), Pagani (Pagans), or Normanni (Northmen).

In 793 A.D., a band of Norsemen attacked the monastery of Lindisfarne - an important religious center in the Kingdom of Northumbria in England. It was the first recorded account of a Viking raid where monks were slaughtered by the Viking warriors to steal treasures, food, and slaves. It was the first among the series of attacks launched by the ruthless pirates who later attacked the early English kingdoms for the next several years.

Certainly, the Vikings proved to be very ruthless, but this is only the case if we judge their deeds based on Christian perspective. For Vikings, as you will later understand, dying in battle is the highest form of religious deed as they will be permitted the opportunity to visit Odin in Valhalla.

It is important to understand that the historical records of Viking attacks were written by Christian chroniclers who were threatened by their raids. Hence, they are naturally demonized in these accounts. For instance, Abbot Alcuin of York dramatically recorded the attack on Lindisfarne. Based on his account "the church was spattered with the blood of priests of God, despoiled of all its ornaments...given as a prey to pagans."

But there is more to the Vikings beyond their destructive and violent raids. Apart from their distinctive brutish attacks, they were also well-versed in trading. In fact, many Norse folk reached as far as Russia to trade goods. They were also the pioneers in sea voyage with their efficiently crafted long ships that navigated the Atlantic, and even reached North America hundreds of years ahead of Christopher Columbus.

Among the Viking ranks included artists who crafted sophisticated jewelry, crafts, and other works of art. Many of them poets who composed the verses and sagas that we can still read today.

Viking Agriculture

While the Vikings are renowned for their fierce raids and sea voyages, the men and women are also expert in tending to their livestock and farms. Men were not expected to battle every day, so they spend most time of their year working in farmstead so they can stock up on food and other essential supplies for winter.

While men were expected to tend the farm, the women typically took care of the home. They would fashion clothes, prepare food for the family, and take care of the children. In some cases, women would be required to care over the entire property, especially whilst the men were off on sea voyages. Some women would also participate in raids as shield maidens.

During harvest time, everyone is expected to help in the farm including children who are readily capable of participating in light tasks. However, farm work that is physically demanding such as dunging fields, constructing store houses, or pulling the plow are given to slaves who were more commonly acquired and captured during battles or raids. Criminals of murder or theft could also be punished into slavery. Slaves would be stripped of their human rights and considered similar to the likes of 'cattle'.

Ironworks were considered as specialized crafts and often completed within the farmsteads and only performed when needed. Blacksmiths were present in some settlements but generally asked for goods such as food or clothes in exchange of their services.

While the image of farm work may seem peaceful, it is not for the Vikings. The work was perilous and everything required a lot of effort as some tasks were prepared by hand. During those times, there were no advanced tools to assist the people in their farmwork. On top of that, the Vikings had to face harsh winters. Many of the Viking families had very limited means to survive the winter when farmwork was interrupted by famine, raid, or natural disasters.

As primary means of transport, the Vikings used horses. But for heavier loads, ox wagons and carts were implemented. Skis and sleds were also used during heavy snow.

The Viking Society

The social structure of the Vikings was composed of three classes - earls, free men and women, and slaves.

The earls were the noble class and stand on top of the social strata. Originally, they were chieftains or warlords who had acquired warriors and wealth through battles and raids. When Scandinavian countries transitioned into monarchy, the noble class became aristocrats who were provided with lands.

Under the earls are the free folk who are composed of warriors, farmers who work in their own lands. Other free men and women may choose to work in other farms in exchange for a share in the harvest. Traders, merchants, or soldiers were amongst the ranks of other free folk. The rights and privileges of the free folk were protected under Viking Law.

Viking warriors were fundamentally free men who didn't hold their own land or wealth. They are free to join raids so they could acquire wealth such as gold, and gain favor from warlords so they could potentially be granted with a piece of land.

The patriarch of the Viking family would usually choose to leave most of their inheritance to their firstborns. Hence, many warriors were men who had not received enough inheritance from the family including second and third born men ect.

The slaves were the lowest class in the Viking society. Children of slaves are automatically considered as slaves and are born into the unfortunate circumstance. However, free folk would often become slaves if they were captured in battle or subdued into bankruptcy. The basis for becoming a slave is reciprocity. Vikings believed that anyone who was captured in a raid and has been spared, has been given the gift of life, so he or she should sacrifice freedom in the return of life.

Free folks could become slaves if they lost all their wealth. Those who were poor had the opportunity to sell their freedom to a wealthier person who in return will take care of their material needs. This was the practice for Vikings who had amassed large amount of debt and so they would give up their freedom as a form of payment.

CHAPTER TWO

THE CREATION OF THE WORLD ACCORDING TO NORDIC LORE

Yggdrasil, the giant ash tree that grows from the Well of Urd, is central to the Norse cosmology. The branches of the Yggdrasil hold the Nine Realms, which are the dwellings of the different beings in the Norse World. The Nine Realms are: Asgard (home of the Aesir deities), Midgard (home of humans), Vanaheim (home of the Vanir deities), Jotunheim (home of the jotuns or giants), Niflheim (realm of ice), Muspelheim (realm of fire), Alfheim (realm of elves), Svartalfheim (realm of the dwarves), and Hel (underworld).

Asgard

Asgard is the realm of the Aesir deities or the gods and goddesses belonging to the Aesir tribe. In Norse mythology, this realm is located in the divine heaven and connected to the human realm (Midgard) via the Rainbow Bridge or Bifrost.

The suffix -gard is a reference to the Norse concept of the difference between innangard and uttangard. Innangard means inside the wall, which is considered as orderly, law-abiding, and civilized. On the other hand, uttangard means outside the wall, which is chaotic, anarchic, and wild. Asgard is considered as the model of innangard, while the home of the giants, Jotunheim is the example of uttangard.

Midgard

Midgard is the realm of mortal men. This is where we live. In Norse mythology, this is the only world that is inside the visible realm, as other realms are believed to be in the realm of spirtiuality. Its name is a reference to its location as it is situated between civilized Asgard and wild Jotunheim. The Norse people believed that Jormungand (a giant serpent) lived in the ocean and surrounded Midgard.

Vanaheim

Vanaheim is the realm of the Vanir deities or the gods and goddesses belonging to the Vanir tribe. These deities have a stronger affinity to nature compared to the Aesir deities. Unlike Midgard and Asgard, this dwelling ends with -heim, which means that this world is natural and less civilized than Asgard but not as wild as Jotunheim.

Jotunheim

Jotunheim is the realm of the jotuns or the giants. In Norse mythology, giants are not necessarily large in size like the modern day concept. Jotuns refer to beings that are powerful but despised by humans, as opposed to the gods and goddesses that are also powerful but praised and adored. In the Eddas, this realm is described as a world that is dark, mountainous, and a harsh never-ending winter.

Niflheim

Niflheim is the primordial world of darkness, cold, and ice. It is not necessarily evil, but a natural realm of coldness. It is the opposite world of Muspelheim or the realm of heat and fire. In the Norse cosmology, the giant Ymir was born when the ice from Niflheim and the fire from Muspelheim met in the center of the Giant Gap (Ginnungagap) or the space that used to divide the two opposing realms.

Muspelheim

Muspelheim is the realm of heat and fire. This is the opposite world of Niflheim or the realm of ice.

Alfheim

Alfheim is the home of the elves. The elves in Norse mythology are powerful individuals that also have god-like qualities but they are not worshipped as deities. They are considered as beings of light as they were kindred spirits that can help humans. This realm is believed to be ruled by Freyr, a Vanir goddess.

Svartalfheim

Svartalfheim is the realm of the dwarves who are highly skilled smiths. This world is envisioned as an underground complex composed of mines and forges. Other sources described Svartalfheim as the realm of the black elves or the enemies of the elves of Alfheim.

Hel

Hel is the realm of the goddess Hel and essentially used to refer to the underworld where the souls of those who have done evil in their existence reside. Similar to Tartarus (underworld in Greek Mythology), Hel is believed to be guarded by a giant dog.

Apart from the inhabitants of the Nine Realms, other creatures are also said to dwell in Yggdrasil. According to the Eddic Poem entitled The Song of the Hooded One, the giant ash tree is also home of a giant eagle that perches in the branches of the tree. Meanwhile, the roots are gnawed by a dragon named Nidhogg. There are also four deers named Dain, Dvalin, Duneyr, and Dyranthror.

Nordic Creation Story

The creation story in Norse mythology is considered as one of the most vivid in cosmological literature. Apart from its beautiful plot, the story also offers a glimpse of the Nordic philosophy. Below is the story of how the world was created according to Nordic cosmology:

In the beginning, there was only Ginnungagap, which is a deep abyss that is dark and cold. This gigantic void was situated between Muspelheim (the world of fire) and Niflheim (the world of ice).

The frost from Niflheim and the billowing flames from Muspelheim met in the Great Gap until the ice melted. From the water drops emerged Ymir or the first giant who was both a man and a woman. He had the ability to give birth to more giants that rose from his sweat.

Another being who was spawned in the melting gap was Audhumbla, which was a giant cow that provided nourishment for Ymir. The mythical cow licked the remaining ice until Buri - the first Aesir god - emerged. His son, Bor, married Bestla, who was the daughter of Bolthorn, another giant. Their children were Odin, Vili, and Ve. The firstborn, Odin, became the chief of the Aesir deities.

Midgard (the realm of humans) was created when Odin and his siblings killed Ymir. The giant's skull became the sky and his brains became the clouds. His hair became the trees, and his skin and muscles became the land. His blood became the sea.

After the creation of the new world, the Aesir gods created the first man and woman named Ask and Embla, respectively. The deities also built a fence around Midgard to protect them from the jotuns or giants.

One interesting aspect of the Nordic creation story is that the creation was caused by something. In the beginning chaos and death could cause life. The Nordic cosmology prominently features reciprocity as a fundamental concept of life. The world, from the Nordic viewpoint, is not created out of nothing in contrast with the creation story of Judeo-Christian religion.

Odin and his siblings had to kill Ymir so they could create Midgard. It would be safe to assume that the Vikings were inspired by the concept of chaos as necessary for life to continue.

Furthermore, the creation story of the Norsemen is seen as a cycle and doesn't follow a linear series of events. In the Christian perspective of creation, the world was created in the past, and was only accomplished through the will of one supreme being who holds the power for creation and also destruction. You will learn more about the Nordic perspective of creation as a cycle when we explore Ragnarok.

Life After Death

The Norse religion doesn't have a solid doctrine about life after death. There is no clear image in Norse mythology on where people pass on to when they die. But based on literary and archaeological sources, there are discernible patterns on how the Norsemen perceive the afterlife.

For instance, different literary pieces usually mention Valhalla (the Hall of the Fallen) as a place fallen soldiers go when they die through heroic acts in a battle or war. Valhalla is the great hall by Odin who selects warriors to celebrate with and aid him in the great battle of Ragnarok.

Those who have not achieved heroic feats but lived a moral life are said to go to Folkyang or the Field of the People. This is the great hall of the goddess Freya. But unlike Valhalla, Folkyang is scarcely mentioned in literary sources. Meanwhile, some sources say that those who died at sea are taken underwater in the realm of Ran - a giantess.

Helgafjell or Holy Mountain is another place for people who have not died in battle but also lived a virtuous life. On the other hand, people who died without honor are believed to go to Helheim, which is a cold and dark realm ruled by the Goddess Hel.

It is interesting to note that for Norsemen, dying in bed because of old age or sickness is considered the worst way to die. That is why even those who are in their senior years were willing to follow the skirmishes so they could fight and die with honor and join Odin in Valhalla.

Valhalla

Valhalla is the great hall of Odin - the chief of the Aesir gods. This hall is where he houses the souls of the warriors whom he considers worthy of joining him to celebrate and prepare for the coming of Ragnarok. Based on literary sources, this great hall is located in the middle of Asgard, the home of the Aesir deities.

In the Song of the Hooded One, Valhalla is described as a magnificent place. Its rafters are made of spears and the roof is made of shields. It has hundreds of tables and chairs made of breastplates where heroic warriors feast with the gods. Wolves guard the gates and eagles fly above the hall.

The inhabitants of Valhalla are called the einherjar who fight each other all day to entertain Odin. While they are already dead, they still get wounded and bleed during the daily battles. But each night, the Valkyries tend to their wounds and restore them to their full health so they can join the nightly feast filled with mead and food.

The Valkyries serve the einherjar with meat that comes from a magical boar called Saehrimnir. This boar is butchered every night but rises again each day. The warriors also drink the wonderful mead from the udder of a magical goat called Heidrun.

While Valhalla is considered as a resting place for heroic warriors, the einherjar is still awaiting for their doom. When Ragnarok comes, Odin has to face Fenrir the wolf. At this endtime, the chief god will call upon the mighty warriors to help him despite of the fact that they are already destined to be defeated.

Odin chooses the mighty warriors through the aid of the Valkyries. Those who are not deemed worthy but died in battle are sent to Folkyang or Freya's hall. You should understand that there is no sufficient source that exactly describes the process of becoming worthy to enter Valhalla.

Therefore, the requirements to seek this reward are not explicit. Scholars also believe that the afterlife in Norse mythology is seen as a continuation of life in Midgard and the Norse religion doesn't judge people based on their virtues unlike the Christian concept of Heaven and Hell.

Remember, it was in the 13th century that Snorri Sturluson, the Irish scholar, filled the gaps in the Norse story. This is centuries after Christianity was already widespread in Scandinavia. Snorri is a Catholic scholar so this imagery might be inspired by the Judeo-Christian concept of life after death. It was Snorri who wrote that those who died in battle are taken to Valhalla, while those who died of old age are taken to Hel.

The Valkyries

The Valkyries are depicted as elegant maidens who help Odin choose warriors to Valhalla. There are literary sources depicting Valkyries as sinister maidens who even influence the outcome of battles so they can collect souls. They were not depicted as objective observers in the battlefield as they can choose who will die in battle and even use dark magic to mark those who they desire to fall.

But most sources depict them as beautiful maidens who even develop romantic relationships with mortal men. They are also depicted as noble aides of Odin with the important duty of collecting warriors and serving them in Valhalla.

In one account, it is said that Odin permits Valkyries to transfigure into pretty white swans to visit Midgard. However, if a mortal sees a Valkyrie turning into a swan, the spiritual maiden can no longer return to Valhalla.

In the Eddic poems, there are accounts about how the Valkyries decide who lives in battle. For example, in Njal's Saga, there were 12 Valkyries that were seen before the start of the Battle of Clontarf. They were said to sit at a loom then weaved the tragic fate of doomed warriors.

The depiction was quite sinister as the Valkyries used decapitated heads for loom weights, swords and arrows as beaters, and intestines to weave the loom. In the Volsungasaga, it is said that watching a Valkyrie is like "staring into a flame".

The concept of Valkyries is widespread in Germanic lore. For example, Anglo Saxons also have their own version of Valkyries known as the *wælcyrie* who were female spirits of carnage. Meanwhile, the Celts also had similar entities such as the war deities

CHAPTER THREE

NORSE GODS AND GODDESSES

The Norse deities usually belong to one of the two divine tribes - the Aesir and the Vanir.

Aesir Gods and Goddesses

Many of the Norse gods and goddesses that we know are members of the Aesir tribe. This includes Odin, Thor, Loki, Frigg, Tyr, Heimdall, and Baldur. Asgard is their home, which is located on the highest branch of Yggdrasil.

Odin

Odin (also known as Woden or Wotan in some literary sources) is the chief of the Aesir deities. However, he can be identified both as an Aesir and Vanir. His mother, Bestla, is in fact a giantess, so he also is of giant blood. One Edda describes him as the life bringer.

The wolf and the raven are sacred to Odin. He also has a magical horse known as Sleipnir. This mythical horse is described as having eight legs and its teeth is inscribed with runes.

The Allfather is depicted as an old man with grey-flowing beard. He only has one eye as he traded his other eye in exchange of wisdom. He is said to carry a spear and wears a cloak and wide-brimmed hat.

While he is the ruler of Asgard, he spends most of his time far from the majestic realm to go wandering alone in Midgard seeking wisdom. He is also an enigmatic god because while he is venerated as a patron of rulers, he is also the god of outcasts. Odin is a fierce god of war and in contrast also the god of poetry.

Thor

Thor is the Norse thunder god that is worshipped by the Vikings because of his honor, loyalty, and brawn. He is known as the strongest defender of Asgard and its divine inhabitants against the jotuns.

As the thunder god, Thor is blessed with unmatched physical strength, which he can double if he is wearing a magical belt known as *megingjarðar.* However, he is best known for his magical hammer known as *m*jöllnir. Thor embodies thunder, while his hammer embodies lightning. His archenemy is Jormungand - a giant snake that encroached Midgard.

While Thor is the defender against the giants, he himself has giant blood. Odin, his father, is half-giant, while Jord, his mother fully descended from the giants. But this ancestry is not uncommon among the Norse gods.

Tyr

Tyr is the old god of war and considered as the Lawgiver among the Asgardians. The most courageous among the Norse pantheon, it is Tyr who bound Fenrir where he lost his right hand. The gods were worried that the pup Fenrir was quickly growing, so they decided to tie up the wolf pup in fetters.

When Fenrir saw the chain that would bind him, he was suspicious, and declared that he will only be bound if one of them would lay an arm in his mouth as a symbol of good faith. As the bravest god, only Tyr agreed to do so. When Fenrir was constrained and failed to break free from the chains, he bit off the arm of the war god.

Before Odin, Tyr was considered as the chief of the Aesir gods. The reason for his demotion is unknown.

Similar to Odin, Tyr has many traits of the early Germanic deities of war. Mentions in other mythologies and archeological evidences related to a one-hand deity, suggest that the character is quite old and has been worshipped in Northern Europe several thousands of years before Snorri Sturluson mentioned the god in the Prose Edda.

Loki

Loki is known as the trickster god in Norse mythology. But technically, Loki is not a god but a Jotun or a giant. While he is not good, he is also not evil. Loki lives in Asgard, and originated from Jotunheim or the realms of the giants. He was the son of Laufey and Farbauti who are both giants. Tricking and annoying the Aesir gods and goddesses is

Loki's entertainment and considers himself as quite a trickster.

The Vikings call Loki the sly one because he is cunning and clever. He is creative in coming up with new ideas to trick and embarrass the gods as well as mortal beings. For the sake of fun, Loki loves to prank people, but will later save them so he will look like the hero.

One of his major powers is shapeshifting into any form he wants. In literary sources, he was noted to transform into an elderly woman, a fly, a seal, a horse, and a salmon.

Loki and Sigyn have two children - Vali and Narvi. But Loki was also married to the giantess Angrboda who gave her three offspring - Jormungand (the archenemy of Thor), Fenrir the Wolf, and Hel the goddess of the underworld. Loki is also considered as a mother as he gave birth to Sleipnir, the magical horse of Odin.

Frigg

Frigg, also known as Frigga, is the most venerated goddess in Norse Mythology. She is the wife of Odin and as such she is allowed to sit on the Allfather's Hlidskjalf or high seat to look out over the universe. She is the mother to the beloved god Baldur and the blind god Hod. She is also the stepmother to Vali, Vidar, Bragi, Tyr, Hermod, Hoder, Heimdall, and Thor.

Frigg is described as a volva that practices seidr or a type of Norse magic related to discerning destiny. She is considered as the goddess of motherhood, fertility, marriage, and love.

According to Norse lore, Frigg has three beloved maidens, but her favorite is Fulla whom she entrusts her secrets. Fulla is depicted as a lovely maiden wearing a golden snood that she recieved as a present from Frigga.

Another maiden is called Gna or the messenger maiden. Her task is to run errands for Frigga all around the Nine Realms. If she needs to deliver an urgent message, she rides Hofvarpnir, another magical horse that can gallop through the ocean. The third maiden is named Hlin whose task is to protect any person or object that is special to Frigg.

Baldur

Baldur, also known as Balder or Baldr, is known as the god of light in Norse mythology. He is well-loved by both the Aesir and Vanir gods, and he is worshipped for his purity. He is the most beautiful god that even the flowers bow down before him. Among the gods, he is the most gracious, most fairest, and wisest.

Balder is the second son of Frigg and Odin. He is the brother of Thor, and the husband of the goddess Nanna and together they bore the god Forseti. Breidablik is the hall of Baldur, which is known as the brightest house in Asgard. It is said that only the purest beings can enter Baldur's hall.

The Eddic poems describe the roof of Baldur's hall as made of silver and emanating from gorgeous pillars. Baldur owns a ship known as Hringhorn that was described as the most beautiful ship in Asgard. During his death, the ship was used as his funeral pyre.

Baldur's death is among the most popular stories in Norse mythology, which you will later read in this book.

Heimdall

Heimdall is another Aesir god who lives in Asgard. However, he has a particular dwelling known as Himinbjoirg that is said to be located at the highest point in Asgard known as Bifrost. He is the guardian of Asgard and armed with the Gjallarhorn or the yelling horn that is blown by the god if there are approaching intruders against Asgard. The sound of this great horn is said to be heard throughout the nine realms.

Idun

Idun is an Aesir goddess, but there is limited information about her. The only source that prominently mentions her is the story about her kidnapping. In the skaddic tale, Idun is noted as the owner and dispenser of an apple tree that bestows immortality. As such she plays an important role in sustaining the immortality of the Asgardians. The husband of Idun is Bragi, the minstrel and court poet of Asgard.

Bragi

Bragi is considered as the god of poetry and songs who entertain the inhabitants of Asgard, especially Odin and his warriors in Valhalla. However, there are some sources that lay doubt on the status of Bragi as a god, as he is considered as a special being among the immortals because of his talent in reciting poetry.

Vili and Ve

Vili and Ve are the two brothers of Odin who played a critical role in the shaping of the Nine Realms. The Eddic Poems tell us that the three brothers were the original Aesir gods to exist who slew the giant Ymir and caused the creation of Midgard. However, other scholars believe that Vili, Ve, and Odin are actually one god only in three forms as these names were used interchangeably in many literary resources.

Forseti

The Vikings regard Forseti as the divine law speaker or the god of justice. He is the son of the goddess Nanna and the god Baldur. He dwells in the shining hall of Glitnir with its roof inlaid with decorative silver and the pillars are made of red gold. This hall serves as his court of justice where he settles legal disputes in Asgard. While Forseti is among the major gods of Norse mythology, he is not significantly featured in any of the surviving literary sources.

Gevjun

Gevjun is considered as the goddess of prosperity, abundance, fertility, and agriculture. Her name can be translated as the Generous One or the Giver. In the account of Snorri Sturluson, the goddess visited the modern-day country of Sweden as a homeless woman. She encountered King Gylfi who was noted for his generosity. The King promised to grant her as much land as four oxen can plow in a day, so the deity called her four sons and turned them into oxen to plow the land.

Not only did the divine sons plow the land, they also dragged the land from Sweden resulting in a depression and became the Malaren Lake. The land stretched out into the ocean and became the island of Zealand, which is now the location of Copenhagen.

Sif

Sif is known as the wife of the thunder god, Thor. Whilst her husband is more popular, Sif was a revered goddess in the pre-Christian Europe as she was worshipped as a goddess of family, fertility, and wheat. The two primary literary sources that describe Sif are the Prose Edda and the Poetic Edda. She is depicted as a beautiful lady with golden hair.

Thor was her second husband as she was first married to Orvandil, who was a giant. She is usually compared to other fertility goddesses such as Frigg and Freya. In the Eddas, Thor was said to be heavily in love with the goddess, especially her beautiful hair. Bright like the sun, flowing flawlessly down her back.

Ullr

Ullr is the son of Sif, the goddess of fertility and wheat, and the stepson of Thor, the thunder god. While the giant Orvandil was the first husband of Sif, there is no existing literary or archaeological evidence that mention the giant as Ullr's father.

Norse scholars establish that this Norse god is another war god that is well-skilled in hunting, archery, and skiing. The Poetic Edda also mentions that his home is known as Ydalir of Yew Dales. In crafting bows, Yew is the preferred wood, which possibly explains this association.

Hermod

Hermod is another war god in Norse mythology, although not as prominent as Odin, Thor, or Tyr. He is the son of Odin and Frigg, and while he is considered as a minor god, he is still a popular one because of the role he played in the story of Baldur's death. When the god of light was killed due to the mischief of Loki, he was the only god in Asgard brave enough to journey to the underworld and encourage Hel to let go of Baldur.

Sigyn

Sigyn is an Aesir goddess and the wife of Loki, the trickster god. Their sons are Vali and Narfi. One occasion when Loki pushed too much mischief towards the inhabitants of Asgard, Odin punished him to be imprisoned and bound in a cave with a venomous snake dangling over his head. Because of her love to Loki, Sigyn sacrificed her freedom and chose to stay with her husband. Sigyn was required to hold a bowl over Loki's head collect the venom and relieve Loki of the pain.

When the bowl would fill up, Sigyn had to leave the cave to throw away the poison, so some of the drops of venom continue to fall on Loki's head causing him tremendous pain. His pain would tremble in the form of earthquakes in Midgard, the realm of humans. Loki will stay imprisoned until Ragnarok and will seek revenge against Odin.

Vanir Gods and Goddesses

The Vanir are skilled in magic and sorcery and they are particularly talented in predicting the future.

Freya

Freya is considered as the goddess of love, sex, and beauty in Norse mythology. But she is also associated with fertility, sorcery, wealth, war, and death. The Vanir goddess is also associated with lust. In the Eddas, Loki accused Freya of having an affair with all the gods as well as elves, including her brother.

The name Freya means lady in Old Norse, and also written as Freiya, Freja, Froya, or Frua. While she is a Vanir goddess, she lives among the Aesir deities after she was sent by the Vanir deities as a token of truce. The Aesir also sent two deities, Mimir and Honir, to the Vanir. As such, Freya became an honorable deity in Asgard after the war between the Vanir and the Aesir ended.

Freyr

Freyr is the twin brother of Freya, who was depicted in the Eddas as a gorgeous deity and associated with good harvest, wealth, and prosperity. When the war between the Aesir and Vanir ended, Freyr with his sister Freya and his father Njord were sent to Asgard as a token of peace. Freyr is also the Lord of the Elves and he reigns in Alfheim, the realm of the Elves. His wife is the giantess Gerd from Jotunheim.

Njord

Njord is a Vanir god that is associated with wealth, inland waters, coasts, seafarers, and wind. Together with his children, Freyr and Freya, the Vanir sent him to the Aesir tribe of gods as a token of truce. He lives in a house near a coast in Asgard named Noatun or Ship Haven.

While Njord is married to the giantess Skadi, he slept with his sister named Nerthus and together they had two children - Freyr and Freyr. Njord is often mistaken as the god of the sea, which is not accurate because the Nordic people worshipped Aegir as the sea god.

Nerthus

Nerthus is a popular Germanic deity that is associated with fertility. This goddess is depicted by Tacitus, a Roman historian from the 1st century AD in his work Germania. In the ethnographic work of Tacitus, he mentioned the union of the Suebi tribes as they venerated the goddess Nerthus by maintaining a sacred grove and a holy wagon draped with cloth that only priests could touch.

The presence of the goddess is said to dwell in the wagon that is drawn by the heifers. The sacred wagon is paraded in towns where people would welcome the group with peace and celebration. All arms are locked away, so there will be no conflict.

However, the culmination of this peaceful celebration is horrifying as the cart and the cloth are washed by the slaves in a secluded lake. The slaves are then sacrificed by the priests by drowning.

Jotuns (Giants)

While the ancient Nordic peoples mainly worshipped the Aesir and the Vanir gods and goddesses, they also believe in the existence of the giants who are equally powerful as the gods. However, the character of the giants are quite different from the deities and in fact, they are seen as opposing yet intertwined forces that balanced the cosmology.

While these beings are called giants, they are not necessarily enormous in size like what we usually think about when we hear the term. In fact, the name giant in reference to the beings who dwell in Jotunheim is a misleading name. In modern English, a giant is a being that is enormous in size. But during the Viking times, the word giant is used to refer to a being that is powerful but dreaded as opposed to the gods that are powerful but adored.

In Old Norse, the giants are called jotnar or jotun. When England was conquered by William the Conqueror in 1066 AD, the English language was filled with Norman (French) terms. One of the terms that were used during those times was the Old French geant, which is the origin of the modern English term giant. This replaced the Old English word jotun.

Geant was used to refer to the giants in the Greek myth who were also the enemies of the gods similar to the jotun in Norse. The Greek origin of geant was also used to translate a Hebrew term that refers to beings that are huge in physical size. And so, this became the dominant meaning of the word.

Below are the prominent giants in Norse mythology.

Ymir

Ymir is a giant that played an important role in the Norse cosmology. Based on the account of the medieval scholar Snorri Sturluson, the giant Ymir was born when the ice from Niflheim and the fire from Muspelheim met in the abyss of Ginnungagap.

The second being to be created in the melting spot was Audhumbla or a cow that nourished Ymir. Audhumbla licked the ice until the first Aesir god, Buri, emerged. Bor, the son of Buri, married Bestla, the daughter of Bolthorn the giant. The couple had children named Odin, Vili and Ve. Odin became the chief of the Aesir tribe gods.

The world was created when Odin and his siblings slew Ymir. The sky was made from his skull, his brains became the clouds, his hair became the trees and plants, his muscles and skin became the land, and his blood turned into ocean. The gods then created the first man and woman named Ask and Embla, and they have constructed a fence around their homeland, Midgard, to protect them from the realm of the giants.

Skadi

Skadi, also known as Skathi, Skadhi, or Skade, is a frost giantess and often associated with winter. Her husband is the Vanir god Njord. When the Aesir gods killed her father, Thiazi, she attacked Asgard to take revenge. To avoid further conflict, the gods proposed a marriage with one of the gods. Skadi was free to choose any god she like, but can only choose based on the appearance of their feet.

She selected the most beautiful pair of feet thinking they were the feet of the handsome god Baldur. However, it turned out that the feet belonged to Njord a less handsome and older Vanir god of the wind.

Skadi is often portrayed as a winter huntress wearing skis or snowshoes. She is also a sorceress, but she is not an evil goddess.

Fenrir

Fenrir is not a pure blood giant. He is the son of the god Loki and Angrboda who was a giantess. Hence, he is the brother of the goddess Hel and the serpent Jormungand - the archenemy of Thor. While he is not a pure blood giant, he is considered as the most prominent giant because he is seen as the doom of the gods who will wreak havoc in the Nine Realms when Ragnarok comes.

Hel

Although technically a goddess, Hel is identified as a giantess who rules over the underworld that is also called Hel. Her father is the trickster god Loki and the giantess Angrboda being her mother. Thus, she is the sister of the world serpent Jormungand and the wolf Fenrir.

The goddess of the underworld is often depicted as indifferent, cruel, harsh, and greedy. However, there is no elaborate description of the goddess in the surviving Norse literature, and she is only mentioned passively in major stories. She is described as being half-white and half-black, with a fierce yet grim facial expression.

Hel played a prominent role in the legend of the Death of Baldur. After the death of the god of light, the stricken Asgardians ordered the god Hermod to quickly travel to the underworld to ask the goddess Hel if there is any chance to resurrect the god of light. When Hermod arrived at Hel, he found Baldur, now grim and pale, sitting in the seat of honor next to the goddess of the underworld.

Hermod asked the goddess to let go of Baldur, and after much encouragement, the goddess agreed to retrieve Baldur if everything in the world would cry for Baldur, to prove the divine claim that the god is universally beloved.

Baldur's mother, the goddess Frigg, quickly travelled around the world to ask everything to weep for the brightest god, and indeed everything wept, except for the giantess named

Þokk, who was assumed to be Loki himself. And so, Baldur remains in Hel until the day of Ragnarok comes.

Jormungand

Jormungand is known as the Midgard Serpent or a Dragon who encircles the realm of the mortal humans. He is an enormous being and he is one of the three children of the giantess Angrboda and the trickster god Loki. His siblings are Hel and Fenrir.

His archenemy is Thor the god of thunder. The Eddas are filled with stories about the battles between Jormungand and Thor. In one story, Thor caught the giant serpent but fails to pull him up when Hymir (a giant) was worried that it will cause Ragnarok. He cuts the line and sends back the serpent to the ocean. It is destined that when Ragnarok comes, the two enemies will kill each other in an epic duel.

The Aesir-Vanir War

In Norse Mythology, the Aesir deities and the Vanir deities have a harmonious relationship with each other. The jotuns or the devourers were their common enemy. But according to literary sources, the two divine tribes were once at war.

Freya, a Vanir goddess, was the most adept practitioner of seidr, a form of powerful magic. As a practitioner of this magic, the goddess wandered around the realms to continuously develop her craft.

One day, he came to Asgard under the name Heiðr, which means "bright". The Aesir was delighted by the power of the goddess and they offered to hire her services to achieve their goals. However, they realized that their values of obedience to the law and honor were being set aside because of their desires through magic.

They blamed the Vanir goddess for tempting them, and they called her Gullveig or one that is greedy with gold and they tried to kill her. They tried to burn her three times but she continued to rise from the ashes each time.

It was the start of conflict between the Aesir and the Vanir, which escalated to a full-blown war. The Vanir used magic to fight while the Aesir used combat and weapons. The war went on with back and forth victories, but there was no clear winner overall.

Eventually, the deities realized they are equal in strength and power, and so they called on a truce. It was customary for Germanic and Norse peoples for the two warring sides to pay tribute by sending hostages to live among each other. The Aesir gods Hoenir and Mimir went to live with the Vanir, while the Aesir deities Njord, Freyr and Freya went to the Aesir.

The Vanir hostages learned to live peacefully with the Aesir. On the other hand, the Aesir hostages found it difficult to live in Vanaheim or the realm of the Vanir. Hoenir is a god of wisdom that can provide advice to any problem. The Vanir thought this will be helpful for them, but they failed to realize that the god can only provide advice if Mimir is around.

When the Vanir realized this, they decapitated Mimir and sent back the head to Odin. The Allfather embalmed the head in herbs and offered enchantments that preserved the head of the god. As such, the severed head was still able to provide advice to Odin when he needed counsel.

But instead of renewing hostilities, the Vanir and the Aesir met again and decided to spit in a pot. From their saliva, a creature emerged and called Kvasir, which was blessed with wisdom as a way of sustaining harmony in the Nine Realms. You will later learn more about the tragic story of Kvasir in the Mead of Poetry.

CHAPTER FOUR

TALES OF NORSE MYTHOLOGY

The Mead of Poetry

The Mead of Poetry is the story of how Odin, the Allfather, searched and possessed the Mead of Poetry.

As you have learned in the previous chapter, the Aesir and the Vanir deities agreed to end their hostilities by spitting into a large pot. From their saliva they created a being called Kvasir. Kvasir was blessed with great wisdom. It is said that no one was able to present him with a problem or a question that he could not answer. Because of his great wisdom, he became popular in the Nine Realms and was highly sought after by other beings.

However, not all beings had good intentions for Kvasir. The two dwarves Galar and Fjalar invited the wisest man to their realm. But upon his arrival, the dwarves killed Kvasir and used his blood to brew mead. This mead contained the ability of Kvasir to dispense wisdom and was named the Mead of Poetry. Anyone who drinks the mead is imbued with wisdom befitting of a great scholar or poet.

The deities realized that Kvasir was no longer present around the Nine Realms and they went to question the two dwarves about the disappearance of Kvasir. However, Galar and Fjalar lied about his death and informed the deities that Kvasir had choked and died.

Apparently, the two dwarves found delight in murder. After slaughtering Kvasir, they enticed the giant Gilling to meet them at the seaside and drowned him for their pleasure. Gilling's wife cried loudly and her weeping irritated the dwarves so they also slaughtered her by dropping a stone on her head.

When Gilling's son Suttung, discovered about the fate of his parents, he entrapped the dwarves and carried them to the reef during low tide, with the intention of them drowning at the rise of tide. The dwarves persistently begged for their lives, and Suttung (who was already aware of the Mead of Poetry) released them on the condition that they will turn over the possession of the mead to him.

After possessing the Mead of Poetry, Suttung hid it under a mountain known as Hnitbjorg and ordered his daughter named Gunnlod to guard the treasure.

Odin eventually learned about the Mead of Poetry and decided he wished to possess it as part of his desire to pursue additional wisdom. Odin was very displeased to find Kvasir was horribly slaughtered, and his abilities of great wisdom lie idle under the mountain of Hnitbjorg.

Disguised as a farmworker, Odin visited the farm of Baugi (the brother of Suttung). He found nine farmhands mowing hay using dull scythes. He approached the the farmhands and offered to sharpen their scythes with his whetstone. The workers agreed not knowing that Odin's whetstone was magical. The scythes became incredibly sharp and were able to cut the hay with ease to the worker's delight.

Together they agreed that the whetstone was the finest that they had seen and asked to buy it from Odin. The god agreed but warned that it bares a high price. Odin threw the whetstone into the air, and witnessed the farm workers scramble to catch the enchanted whetstone. The workers fought each other to the death with their newly sharp scythes in an attempt to wield such a magical tool.

After the gruesome scene, Odin proceeded to Baugi's home. Introducing himself as Bolverker, Odin offered to do the work of the nine servants who he had previously met and witness slaughter themselves. In exchange of his services, he asked to take a sip from the Mead of Poetry.

Baugi replied that he is not in possession of the Mead and that his brother guards it carefully. However, Baugi promised that if Bolverker can really perform the work of the nine farmhands, he would help him acquire the Mead.

With Odin's divine powers, he was able to fulfill his promise to Baugi, who agreed to traverse with him to Suttung's home and ask about the mead. However, upon arrival Suttung angrily refused.

Odin reminded Baugi of their agreement and persuaded the giant to help him to gain access to the mountain where the Mead was hidden. And so, the giant drilled a hole into the mountain. When the task was complete, Odin shape shifted into a snake and crawled into the hole.

While Odin was inside the mountain, he transformed into a young, handsome man to lure the giantess Gunnlod. Odin successfully woo'd the giantess with her agreeing to give him three sips of the Mead on the condition he would sleep with her for three nights. On the third night, Odin went to the mead and greedily drank the entirety of the bottle. He subsequently shape shifted into a giant eagle and escaped the mountain to return to Asgard. Upon learning about the trickery, Suttung similarly shape shifted into a giant eagle to pursue Odin.

When the Aesir deities noticed that their chief was flying to Asgard with a jotun behind him, they fortified the gates of Asgard. Odin was able to reach the divine realm before the jotun could catch him. Suttung retreated in a rage of anger.

Odin brought forth a vessel and regurgitated the mead into it. However, several drops fell from his mouth dripping down to Midgard, the realm of humans. These drops are said to be the source of the abilities of mediocre scholars and poets.

Loki and the Dwarves

Loki, the trickster god, is notorious for his mischief. Many of his acts were done for mere pleasure. One day, Loki found himself in great desire to cut the gorgeous golden hair of the goddess Sif, the wife of the thunder god, Thor.

Upon learning of this mischief, Thor was enraged and seized Loki threatening him to break his bones. The sly god begged for his life, and promised to go into Svartalfheim (the realm of the dwarves) to ask if they could spin a new head of golden hair for the goddess. Thor, who loved his wife dearly, permitted the sly god to traverse immediately to the home of the dwarves.

Blessed with high persuasion skills, Loki was able to obtain all that he promised to Thor. In Svartalfheim, the sons of the master dwarf Ivaldi created not only a new head of golden hair for Sif but also two additional gifts for Thor. Firstly, Gungnir; a spear that wields awe-inspiring powers. Secondly, the Skidbladnir; a mighty ship that is always favored by the winds and holds the power to be folded into a pocket sized gadget.

Loki was amazed by the craftsmanship of the dwarves that he stayed a bit longer than originally intended. He then journeyed to the brothers Sindri and Brokkr teasing that they could never create innovative creations that could equal or surpass the treasures forged by the sons of Ivaldi. He was so certain that he even bet his own head. However, the brothers accepted the challenge.

Loki, nervous that he may lose his own bet, transformed into a fly and stung the hand of Sindri when the dwarf commenced work. But his effort to trick and hinder the dwarf came into no effect as Sindri was still able to reveal his creation. The innovative invention was a magical boar with golden hair. The boar was named Gullinbursti who could emit light in the dark and maneuver through air and water.

After the first conception, Sindri continued working on a third project while Brokkr worked to complete his creation to prove Loki wrong. In another attempt to delay the dwarves, Loki bit Brokkr on the neck to no avail. The second creation was finished and dwarf unveiled a magical ring called Draupner. The ring had the power to multiply and replicate itself every nine days.

For the third and final creation, Sindri worked with the material iron and told his brother that for this piece, they should be very careful for any error would be considerably more expensive in comparison to the first two creations. The fly once again bit the eyelid of Brokkr, and the dripping blood blocked Brokkr's vision preventing him to accurately perceive the work ahead of him.

The brothers eventually through all the distractions forged a hammer that was so powerful that it could never miss its target and would return to its owner once thrown. The hammers handle was crafted short to Sindri's disappointment. Sindri cried that this misfortune ruined his masterpiece. This hammer crafted by the dwarf brothers is what we know of today as Mjolnir. Nonetheless, the masterpieces were so spectacular that the brothers voyaged behind Loki to Asgard to present them to the Aesir deities in person.

As promised, Loki delivered the new head of golden hair to Sif, and for Thor he gifted Mjolnir. Odin received the Gungnir spear and the Draupner ring, while Freyr received Gullinbursti and Skidbladnir.

The Aesir gods were extremely grateful to the dwarves for these gifts, and mutually agreed with the dwarves that Loki should give his head for losing the wager. When the brothers approached Loki to claim his head, the sly god declared that he only promised his head and not his neck. So Sindri and Brokkr sewed the sly god's mouth and returned to their home in disgust.

The Fortification of Asgard

Asgard, the home of the Aesir gods and goddesses, is protected by a high wall, which defends the Aesir from the attacks of the jotuns and other enemies of the gods. However, this protective wall wasn't always present. This story narrates the tale of how the wall was constructed - and is considered as one of the most scandalous and raunchiest stories among mythological lore.

One day, an unknown smith visited Asgard to offer his services of building a high wall to protect and fortify the Aesir deities. The smith, who was said to be a jotun, promised to complete the work in only three seasons, but in exchange, he asked for a high compensation. He asked to be married to the goddess Freya, as well as the right to the sun and the moon.

The wall will be an important fortification for Asgard, so the gods discussed the proposal of the smith. Freya was of course against the proposal, but Loki suggested that the smith be granted his wish, only if he can complete the work in a single winter with no assistance from anyone but his horse.

After a lengthy discussion, the gods agreed to the plan of the sly god. Certainly, the gods did not wish to lose Freya, nor did they desire to part with the sun and moon. With so much to lose the gods and goddesses made certain the task would be near impossible to complete.

To their surprise, the smith agreed to the revised terms, and demanded that the gods swear oaths to make certain that they will fulfill the bargain, and also to protect himself while working in Asgard.

The smith began manufacturing the wall, and the Aesir deities marveled at how fast the wall was erected. The smith's horse, named Svadilfari, was equally spectacular as it was able to haul large boulders from faraway distances to add to the structure.

When the end of winter was nearing, the wall was strong and close to completion. The smith only had to add the final boulders around the gate to finalize the fortification. Odin seized Loki and blamed him for giving them bad counsel. He threatened to kill him if he couldn't look for a way to prevent the smith from completing the task.

The gods were not willing to give away Freya. Also, offering the sun and moon to the giant smith will cause darkness to the Nine Realms. Loki apologetically begged for his life, and promised that he would find a way.

Later that night, the smith and his horse journeyed once again into the snowy forest to look for the perfect boulders. While on their way, a mare, who was Loki in disguise, lured the stallion. The horse immediately galloped after the mare and chased Loki. When morning came, and the horse still missing, the giant inconsolably realized that there would be no way that he could successfully complete his project.

Instead of fulfilling their end of their bargain, the Aesir gods ordered Thor to blow the giant's head into pieces using Mjolnir.

Meanwhile, Svadilfari was able to close in on Loki and impregnate him. Loki gave birth to a horse with eight legs. The newborn foal was named Sleipnir and became the horse of Odin. This is how Loki obtained the label of being a mother.

Why Odin is One-Eyed?

While Odin is considered as the highest divine being in Norse religion, he is not omniscient. Based on literary sources, he still quests for wisdom, and he is willing to pay the price to understand the mysteries of the universe. In his quest to discover the runes, he hanged himself in a branch of Yggdrasil, with a spear wound, and fasted for nine days.

In another lore, he is said to have visited the Well of Urd, which nourishes the Yggdrasil. The well is the home of Mimir - a being from the shadows but was imbued with great knowledge of the cosmos. Odin believed that Mimir achieved this status mainly by drinking water from the well.

When Odin asked to drink from the well, Mimir refused unless the Allfather gave one eye in return. Of all the things in the Universe, Odin seeks wisdom, so he gouged his eye and dropped it into the well without hesitation. With this divine sacrifice, Mimir dipped a horn into the well so the one-eye god could take a sip of the cosmic draught.

Odin's Discovery of the Runes

As evident in the previous tale, Odin is relentless in seeking cosmic wisdom. He is also willing to sacrifice anything for this endless desire. The story of how the Allfather discovered the runes is another strong indication of his convincing desire to understand the mysteries of the universe. It also demonstrates his unyielding willpower.

The runes refer to the written letters used by the Norse prior to the usage of Latin letters in the Middle Ages. Not similar to the Latin script, which is basically a utilitarian alphabet, the runes symbolize powerful forces or magic. As a matter of fact, the term "rune" means mystery.

With deep knowledge of the runes, anyone can interact with the magical forces of the cosmos. Hence, when Odin pursued the runes, he wasn't merely trying to obtain a set of random symbols or sounds. Instead, he was seeking a power that is worthy for the divine.

As you should know by now, the great tree of Yggdrasil is at the center of the Norse cosmology. Its upper branches support Asgard, which is the home of the Aesir deities, of whom Odin is the king.

The Well of Urd nourishes Yggdrasil. This well is vast and deep and holds many powerful beings in the universe. Among these powerful beings are the Norns - who are three wise maidens shaping the fate of all beings. The methods they use to form the fate is by carving runes into the trunk of the Yggdrasil. These runes carry the intentions throughout the tree that impacts the fate of all those living in the Nine Realms.

Odin, a relentless seeker of wisdom, examined the Norns from Asgard and developed jealously of their wisdom and powers. He decided to educate himself and further study the magical powers of the runes.

The native origin of the runes is located in the Well of Urd, and the runes do not haphazardly reveal to anyone who are not worthy. Odin had to hang himself in Yggdrasil while pierced with a spear. While in this position, he observed the shadowy waters of the well. To prove his worth, he mandated the other deities not to help him in any form. And so he bent his will and invoked the power of the runes.

He remained hanging in the great tree for nine days and nine nights. At the end of day nine, he finally discovered the shapes in the well. The runes accepted his sacrifice and revealed themselves to the chief of the gods, offering to him not only their symbols but also their meanings.

Discovering the knowledge of the runes, Odin transformed to be among the most powerful beings in the universe. He also learned runic chants that bestowed him with more powers such as how to accomplish love, wake the dead, protect his comrades in battle, expose and defeat practitioners of dark magic, put out fires, free himself from constraints, bind his enemies, and heal bodily and emotional wounds.

The Kidnapping of Idun

Idun is a goddess who lives in Asgard. While she is considered as a minor deity, she fulfilled an important role as she was the guardian of the mystical apples that enabled the gods to preserve their youth. The story about her kidnapping is among the most prominent tales in Norse mythology.

One day, three Aesir deities - Hoenir, Loki, and Odin took on a long journey. When they reached a desolate mountain, the trio stopped to find food. However, the place was devoid of edible plants, so when they came upon a herd of oxen, they killed one for their meal.

However, when the deities heated the meat over the fire, it failed to cook regardless of the fire's intensity, or the duration they cooked the meat. Suddenly, they heard a voice above them from a large eagle perched on a tree.

The eagle said that he is the one preventing the meat from being cooked through magic. The mystical eagle said that he will release the spell if the gods give him a share of their food. While irritated, the gods agreed with little to no choice, staring at the eagle as it flew down and bit the largest portion of the meat available.

Loki found this to be unfair, and so he took a branch from the tree and began ferociously whipping it toward the eagle. The eagle was swift and too quick for him and snatched the branch attached to Loki and flew him high up in the air. The frightened god once again pleaded for his life, but the eagle refused to do so. It turned out the eagle had shape shifted from his original form of a jotun. To escape from the horrifying circumstance, Loki promised that he would deliver the apples of Idun to the jotun named Thjazi.

When the gods returned back to Asgard, Loki immediately visited Idun and lied that he had discovered apples that are far sweeter and mythical than any growing in Asgard. The sly god asked Idun to follow him into the forest and if she should bring her prized apples to compare. Idun agreed to follow Loki, and when they finally reached the forest, the goddess was captured by Thjazi and taken away to his home known as Thrymheim, located in a high mountain peak with icy caps.

Without Idun, the Aesir deities, gradually grasped by old age. Their hair greyed, their skin became wrinkled, and their strength waned. Odin called an emergency meeting and queried the deities about the absence of Idun. It was only then that it was discovered the goddess had been kidnapped by the giant because of Loki's trickery.

The deities seized Loki and forced him to divulge what transpired regarding Idun. Loki pleaded and revealed what he had done. Odin ordered Loki to release Idun and threatened the sly god that if he fails to rescue her that he will be brutally executed.

Freya lent Loki her hawk feathers enabling anyone in possession to shape shift into a hawk to speed up the mission. Loki immediately flew to Jotunheim to find Thrymheim. When he arrived at his destination, he discovered that the giant had sailed out to sea on a fishing voyage, and had left Idun alone. Loki quickly turned Idun into an apple and escaped away from the giant's realm grasping Idun tightly in his talons.

Upon returning from his fishing, Thjazi discovered that Idun was missing. He shape shifted into his eagle form and pursued Loki. The jotun was closing in on the sly god and at the brink of catching him. The Aesir deities noticed the chase, and immediately surrounded the walls with kindling. Still clutching Idun, Loki made it within the barrier, and the gods lit the fire. The kindling exploded into flames, the giant had no time to escape and was burnt to a crisp in mid-air.

The Marriage of Njord and Skadi

The tale about the marriage of Njord and Skadi begins where the Kidnapping of Idun concludes.

While the Aesir deities were in the middle of a celebration in Asgard for their victory against Thjazi and the return of Idun to their realm, an uninvited guest arrived at the hall of the gods.

It was Thjazi's daughter named Skadi, who had arrived in Asgard in full armor to seek vengeance for the demise of her father. The gods could slaughter the giantess with ease but decided to not spill further unnecessary blood. Hence, they were patient with the giantess and bribed her to accept their gifts rather than continuing her revenge.

As part of reparation, Odin took the eyes of Thjazi and mystically cast them into the evening sky where they became bright stars. The giantess was delighted, but declared it was not enough.

Subsequently, the other deities promised to make the giantess laugh. All of the deities tried but to their surprise none of the gods were able to attain even a small giggle out of the giantess. Finally, Loki caught a goat and tied it to one end of a rope, and the other end around his testicles. He started a game of tug of war with the hapless goat. The two howled and screeched until at last Loki fell into the lap of the giantess who then chuckled.

Still, it wasn't enough. Finally, the giantess exclaimed that she will only abandon her will to avenge her father by marrying an inhabitant of Asgard. The gods consented but only agreed if she was to choose her husband with the view of his feet and legs alone. Skadi selected the most beautiful pair of legs amongst the gods, thinking they belonged to the handsome Baldur. But it turned out that those legs belonged to Njord - the god of the sea.

And so, Skadi and Njord were married in Asgard, and their wedding was magnificent. After their wedding, they had to choose a location to settle. Njord's home was a warm, bright place called Noatun. It was the opposite of Skadi's place - Thrymheim, which was a cold and dark place in the mountain peaks where the winter never ends.

They could not choose, so they decided to try living in each other's place for a certain period of time. They first spent nine days and nights in Thrymheim. Njord declared that the place was loathsome. After, they spent nine days and nights in Noatun. Skadi declared that the place was too bright that she found it impossible to sleep. With such indecision Skadi grew tired and the two parted ways.

The Binding of Fenrir

While Loki lives with the Aesir deities in Asgard, he is a jotun, and he had borne children that were terrifying. His marriage to the giantess Angrboda had resulted to three hideous children. The firstborn was Jormungand - the giant snake that encroached Midgard. The second child was Hel - the ruler of the underworld. The third child was the wolf named Fenrir.

The Aesir deities had horrendous premonitions about their fate with the existence of these children. The era of the Aesir gods would later end when Ragnarok strikes, and these beings would play a major role. Jormungand is destined to kill Thor during the end of times that will be caused by the refusal of Hel to release the god Baldur from the underworld. During Ragnarok, Odin is also destined to be devoured by Fenrir the wolf.

To keep these devourers under control, Odin banished Jormungand into the ocean where he encroaches Midgard. On the other hand, Hel was confined to the underworld. Fenrir was the most fearsome, so they closely watched the young wolf. The war god Tyr was the only one who dared to take care of Fenrir.

Because of his jotun blood, Fenrir grew at a disturbing rate, and so the Aesir deities deemed it important that he should leave Asgard shortly. Knowing well how much damage the wolf could cause if they allow him to roam around the Nine Realms, the Aesir gods tried to bind him using enchanted chains.

While Fenrir grew to be quite big of size, his mind was still of a young pup. The gods tricked him into thinking they are binding him to test his strengths. Testing numerous manacles, no restraint could ever bind the jotun wolf.

Odin decided to employ the services of the dwarves, who are among the most skilled craftsmen in the Universe. The dwarves were able to craft a chain that is magnificently robust. This magical chain was crafted from the spittle of a bird, the breath of a fish, the roots of mountains, the beard of a woman, and the footsteps of a cat. These things simply do not exist and so any struggle to be free is futile. The chain was named Gleipnir.

When the Aesir deities presented Fenrir the new chain, the young wolf doubted the intentions of the gods. Hence, he only agreed to try the new chain if a god or a goddess would lay a hand in his jaws as an assurance. Fulfilling an oath is important for the gods, and so no one dared to agree to the terms of Fenrir.

Eventually, Tyr, the indefatigable god volunteered to fulfill Fenrir's demand. So the gods bound Fenrir, and after the wolf was unable to escape from the mystical chain, he chomped off and swallowed the hand of Tyr.

Fenrir was banished into a desolate place, and the chain was bound to a large boulder. The gods lodged a sword between the jaws of the wolf so they would remain open and pose little threat. He is believed to stay in that state until Ragnarok arrives.

The Tale of Utgarda-Loki

One day, Thor and Loki went on a journey pulled by the goat-drawn chariot of Thor. At night, they found a home of a farmer where they were welcomed as guests. In exchange for their warm hospitality, Thor slaughtered his goats so they could all enjoy a sumptuous dinner. These goats embraced magical powers enabling Thor to bring them back to life again. When the group were finished with supper, Thor placed the hides on the floor and instructed the hosts to lay the bones on the hides.

The farmer had two children - a daughter named Roskva and a son named Thjalfi. In spite of Thor's strict instruction, the boy broke the leg bones of the goats to sip on the marrow.

The following morning, Thor brought the goats back to life. However, one of them had a lame leg. Thor instantly suspected what had happened, and became angry. He threatened to kill the family, but the farmer pleaded for their lives and instead offered him his children for servitude. Hence, Roskva and Thjalfi became the servants of Thor.

And so the two gods and the two children proceeded with the journey to reach Jotunheim, crossing wide seas and thick forests along the way. At night, they discovered an abandoned hall and decided to settle for the night.

During deep sleep, the party was jostled by a strong earthquake. A sleeping giant whose snores could shake and rumble the earth quickly startled them to their feet. Thor, who naturally hated giants, aimed his hammer in anticipation of killing the giant. However, the giant unexpectedly woke up and rumbled out his name; Skrymir. Skrymir boasted that he knew Loki and Thor and explained that he was of no threat.

It turned out that the great hall where Thor and his company settled on was in fact the glove of the giant. The giant later offered to join them on their quest, in which Thor agreed and together they proceeded on with their journey.

When the next night overtook the party, they rested under a large oak tree. Skrymir had been carrying all the party's provisions inside his giant bag and rested on the bag for comfort. Despite of his strength, Thor was unable to open the bag to recover some of his belongings while the giant lay in deep slumber. He became so irritated that he hammered the giant on his forehead so hard thinking he would kill him and his body crumble to dust. However, the giant awoke peacefully scratching his head thinking that a leaf had fallen on him.

Later that night, Skrymir's snore was again so loud that it sounded like enormous thunder strikes. The god of thunder becoming terribly impatient and decided to kill the giant once and for all. Thor hammered Skrymir in the forehead again. But just like before, Skrymir awakened and question the group if a branch had fallen on his forehead.

Just before the break of dawn, Thor tried one final time to kill Skrymir but the giant would conclude to be no match for Thor's powerful hammer. Thor became so irritated that he had no option but to ask Skrymir to depart and refrain from continuing the quest with the group.

The giant graciously agreed and the party continued their voyage towards Jotunheim. The group reached their destination around midday. However, they discovered that the gate was locked and to allowing them passage they would need to break through. With a swift swing of Thor's hammer the locks were disjointed and fell in pieces to the ground.

Upon entering the gate, they discovered a hall with many men merrymaking in celebration. Among them was Utgarda-Loki who was the king of the castle the group had entered. The giant king recognized the gods and laughed at their small size.

Loki sought to save his dignity, so he proudly declared that no one in the castle could win over him in an eating contest. Utgarda-Loki challenged the sly god to prove his assertions through a contest. Loki's opponent was Logi.

The table was filled with meat for the two contenders. Logi was at one end and Loki at the other. The challenge was to get into the middle first by eating through the buffet. After many mouthfuls the two contestants met in the middle exactly at the same time. However, while Loki had only eaten the meat, Logi had also devoured even the bones. Hence, Logi was declared victorious.

Thjalfi, was a fast runner and after Loki's defeat posed a challenge of racing. Utgarda-Loki accepted the challenge and asked his champion named Hugi to compete. Unfortunatley, Hugi was much faster than Thjalfi and he easily reached the end of the line leaving Thjalfi breathless. The two contestants raced three times to test a true result, and Hugi won each time.

Finally, Thor left scratching his head challenged the inhabitants of the castle to a drinking contest. Now, Thor is known for his voracious appetite for drinking, especially mead. Utgarda-Loki ordered a servant to bring a type of drinking horn. When it was presented before the thunder god, the king of the castle informed him that whoever could finish drinking liquor from the horn first will be declared the greatest drinker.

Thor grabbed the horn to skull the mead, but by the time he paused to catch his breath, the level of mead in the horn had replenished. Confused, he drank the mead again. Once again when he paused for a breath, the horn was again refilled with mead to the brim. He tried for the third time and again failed watching as those surrounding him laugh in amusement.

Utgarda-Loki even dared Thor to try lifting his cat, but the thunder god also failed to do so. Clearly irritated, Thor posed another challenge of wrestling. Utgarda-Loki ordered Elli - an old maid servant to wrestle with Thor. But again, the thunder god lost to her in amazement.

After this last challenge, Utgarda-Loki decided to call it a night and the company of Thor will be welcomed as guests in the castle for bringing fourth such great entertainment.

In the morning, Thor and his companions awakened and prepared to depart the castle. But before leaving, Utgarda-Loki summoned the group to reveal what really happened in the challenges the night before.

Utgarda-Loki explained that Loki had in fact done amazingly well in the eating contest, because he was competing against fire itself. Also Thjalfi, was in fact the speed of light and Thjalfi stood no chance. The horn that was used for Thor's drinking challenge was connected to the ocean. Utgarda-Loki was actually frightened that Thor would continue to drink the entirety of the sea. The castle cat was actually Jormungand, and Thor actually wrestled against old age in the final challenge.

Thor was angered by yet another humiliation, that in a rage he endeavored to kill Utgarda-Loki, but the castle suddenly vanished within the blink of an eye and the group stood in awe with nothing in sight, nothing but a vast plain.

The Fishing for Jormungand

One day, the Aesir deities decided to hold a lavish celebration in honor of Ran and Aegir - the deities of the sea. The two sea gods offered to host the banquet, but only on one condition. The gods must provide a giant kettle that is large enough to brew mead for all the guests.

Now, in the whole universe, the gods knew that only Hymir, a giant, possessed a giant kettle that is big enough for the celebration. Thor volunteered to go to the home of Hymir and ask to borrow the giant kettle.

When Thor arrived at Hymir's abode, the giant slaughtered three bulls for the guests dinner. However, the giant was shocked and disappointed when the thunder god ate two whole bulls at once. Thor was known for his big appetite. As such, the angry giant asked Thor to accompany him for a fishing trip in the morning to acquire more food.

The next day, the giant asked Thor to gather fishing bait. The thunder god went to the pasture of the giant and killed the largest bulls so they could use their heads as bait. Hymir was again angered by the action of the brute god, but remained calm as he was hopeful that Thor's strength and determination would be helpful on their fishing trip.

The two boarded the fishing boat, and the thunder god sat in the stern. He rowed the boat out in to the sea, and immediately they hooked two whales. After reeling in the gigantic whales. Thor started rowing the boat further and further out to sea. In foresight of this, Hymir started to become afraid and asked Thor to row back, as the waters ahead were in the realm of Jormungand, the archenemy of Thor.

The thunder god dropped the oars and cast his fishing line into the sea without hesitation. After a short time, Thor felt a strong tug. As he pulled on the line, a violent rumbling shook their fishing boat. Hymir had never been as frightened before, and begged Thor to stop. But the thunder god persisted.

Suddenly, Jormungand's head appeared out from the water, in disbelief Thor quickly reached for his hammer. But the giant cut the line in a surprised panic. Thor missing the opportunity to kill his enemy started to boil with anger. He picked up the giant and tossed him deep out into the ocean, snatched the two whales, voyaged back to Hymir's home, and began the journey back home along with the giant kettle.

Thor the Transvestite

One day, Thor discovered that his powerful hammer, Mjolnir, was missing. It was a critical situation in Asgard, because this mystical hammer (forged by the dwarves) is their most powerful weapon against the jotun or any enemy for that matter. In panic, the deities searched for Mjolnir but failed to locate it in Asgard.

The Vanir goddess Freya possessed mystical falcon feathers that enabled its wearer to transform into a falcon. She lent these feathers to Loki to traverse at a speedily pace to find Mjolnir. The sly god shape shifted into a falcon and flew away to look for the hammer. He instantly thought that the jotuns took the prized possession, so he rode to Jotunheim.

When Loki arrived in Jotunheim, he immediately marched to the king of the giants named Thrym. The sly god demanded about the whereabouts of the hammer. The chief of the jotuns answered that Loki was correct in assuming that the jotuns snatched the hammer and they buried it deep under Jotunheim. He also added that he will only return Mjolnir if the lovely Freya would take his hand in marriage.

Loki returned to Asgard and told this condition to the gods. Naturally, everyone was furious, especially Thor and Freya. After much deliberation, Heimdall suggested a creative and cunning plan. He proposed that Thor could journey to Jotunheim disguised as Freya, find Mjolnir and punish the jotun thieves.

Initially Thor didn't agree because he thought that wearing the robes of a woman would appear unmanly. Furthermore, the backlash and taunting from the other gods would forever haunt him. The thunder god finally consented to the disguise when Loki explained the importance that without Mjolnir, Asgard could soon be under threat by the jotuns. Thor thereby agreed to the plan.

And so the thunder god was dolled up with a lovely dress and transformed into Freya. When Thor was ready, Loki offered to accompany him as a shape shifted maid-servant. The pair travelled in a chariot drawn by goats and together voyaged to Jotunheim. Welcomed by the giant Thrym, with tears of joy in his eyes that at long last the Aesir gods had bowed into his conditions.

During supper, Thor and Loki discovered themselves in a bit of a situation. Thor, with his voracious appetite, easily swallowed an entire roasted oxen and drank a whole barrel of mead and Loki not far behind him. Causing Thrym to become awfully suspicious of the pair, and proclaimed that he had never seen a goddess with such an appetite. Loki reasoned out that Freya (who was actually Thor) was so hungry due to her lovesick for the chief of the jotuns.

Thrym accepted this reason, and asked to kiss his bride. Reaching out for a kiss, Thrym caught the eyes of Thor glaring back at him. An image that could burn a hole. He declared that he had never seen a goddess with such burning eyes. Loki, ever the sly god, reasoned out that Freya wasn't able to sleep well because of her lovesick for the jotun.

The wedding ceremony soon commenced. To bless their union, Thrym ordered Mjolnir to be brought forth. When Thor's hammer was laid on his lap, he immediately grasped the handle and exterminated Thrym including all of the invited jotuns present at the wedding. Loki and Thor hurried back to Asgard. The god of thunder and the sly god changed back into their armored clothes.

Thor's Duel with Hrungnir

Hrungnir was known as one of the mightiest beings among the jotuns. One day, Odin decided to visit this mighty jotun in Jotunheim. At first, Hrungnir failed to recognize the Allfather, and so he questioned the stranger with the loud horse that could ride through water and air.

Upon hearing this insult at his arrival, Odin waged a bet that Sleipnir (the horse he was mounting) is the fastest horse in the

Universe. Hrungnir was irritated by this outrageous statement and accepted this challenge, riding his horse named Gullfaxi.

And so, Odin and Hrungnir raced through thick forests, rocky hills, water, and mud. Before he realized, the race was over and found Odin patiently waiting for him at the finish line. While Hrungnir lost the race by such a dramatic margin, Odin still invited him to drink and celebrate with the gods.

After drinking barrel after barrel of mead, Hrungnir became drunk and lost control. He even declared that he would slaughter all of the gods, except for the goddess Freya and Sif, the wife of Thor. He slurred that he would carry these goddesses back to Jotunheim and that they would become his brides.

Thor heard about the belligerence of the giant. And so, he lifted Mjolnir and prepared to slay the giant right there and then. The giant exclaimed that Thor would be forever branded a coward if he didn't allow a fair fight. Hrungnir added that they should instead duel. As a noble god, Thor accepted the challenge.

During the agreed time and location, Hrungnir arrived wearing a stone shield and used a whetstone for his weapon. Within seconds, Hrungnir heard thunder and began to witness lightning strike from above him, and Thor roared down in front of him. The thunder god threw his hammer with unrelenting force at the jotun, in return Hrungnir whipped his whetstone toward Thor. The stone burst against the head of Thor and broke into many small pieces. It is said that the remnants of the whetstone became the flints scattered around the human realm, Midgard. Mjolnir also struck the giant's head and cause a gigantic blow bringing the giant crumbling down to the ground.

A minute piece of the giant's whetstone was lodged in the head of the thunder god. To speed up the recovery, Thor rushed to a sorceress named Groa who chanted spells over the stone in hopes that it would disappear. While Groa was removing the stone, Thor was encouraged to tell her wonderful stories of his adventures to distract him from the procedure. However, this backfired because Groa was so overjoyed in intrigued that she forgot to complete her chants. And so, the rock remained in the brows of Thor until Ragnarok strikes.

The Death of Baldur

Baldur's death is among the most popular stories in Norse mythology. When the god of light began to dream of his demise, his mother Frigg, travelled around the world to ask from every being (living or non-living) a pledge not to harm her beloved son. As a result, Baldur became invincible. The gods entertained themselves by throwing weapons and any object within reach, but everything just rebounded off him as fulfilment for their promise not to harm the god.

The trickster god Loki sensed a chance for mischief. He visited Frigg and asked if she had overlooked anything when she was asking for the divine pledges. It turned out that the goddess thought that the harmless mistletoe was too insignificant that she skipped asking for a pledge. Knowing suck powerful information Loki fashioned a spear made of mistletoe and persuaded Hodr, the blind god, to throw the weapon toward Baldur. The spear brutally impaled the god, killing him instantly.

The stricken Asgardians ordered the god Hermod to hurriedly travel to the underworld to request the goddess Hel to resurrect the god of light. When Hermod arrived at Hel, he discovered Baldur, now grim and pale, sitting in the seat of honor next to the goddess of the underworld.

Hermod pleaded with the goddess to free Baldur from her grasp, and after much encouragement, the goddess agreed to revive Baldur on one condition. The condition involved every being in the world crying for Baldur, to prove the divine claim that the god was universally beloved.

Understanding the demands of the goddess, Frigg again quickly traversed around the world to ask everything to weep for the brightest god. Indeed, everything wept in sadness for Baldur, except for a giantess named Pokk, who was assumed to be Loki himself in an alternate form. And so, Baldur was to remain in Hel until the day of Ragnarok.

Loki Bound

There is no clear account why Loki, despite of his jotun blood, lives with the Aesir deities in Asgard. In fact, he had always caused a lot of trouble for the gods. He caused a lot of mischief among the gods and even among humans. However, after the damage that he caused surrounding the death of Baldur, Odin decided that he had abused the favor of the gods and had no choice but to punish him severely.

Although, Loki escaped Asgard and fled into a mountain peak, where he built himself an abode with four doors. The four doors allowed Loki to scout anyone incoming from the four directions. During the day, he distorted into a salmon hiding in a nearby river. At night, he would sit by the warmth of fire dreaming of plans to distract the deities if they were to ever find him.

Despite of Loki's efforts to evade Odin, the Allfather eventually managed to discover his location. When Loki saw the Asgard deities approaching the mountain, he set a fishing net on fire to cause distraction and shape shifted back into a salmon to hide away in the rivers depths. When Odin saw the net on fire, he surmised that the sly god was attempting to distract them. The deities immediately weaved their own fishing net and maneuvered toward the river speculating that Loki had transformed into a fish to conceal himself.

The deities tried several times to cast the net into the river, but consistently failed to catch Loki in his scaly salmon form. Finally, Loki bounded out of the water in one leap of faith toward the ocean. But while he was mid-air, Thor threw out his arm and caught the slippery salmon. Loki writhed in the thunder god's grip, but the war god held him tightly by the tail. This is said to be the reason the salmon bares a slim tail.

Captured, the sly god out of options was forced to transform back into his original form. Consequently, Odin brought the two sons of Loki, transforming one child into a wolf who savagely devoured Loki's second son. The gods subsequently bound Loki within three stones inside a cave using the entrails of his slaughtered son. The entrails would be later enchanted by Odin and distorted into hardy iron chains.

The giant Skadi coiled a venomous snake around a rock above Loki's head where it dripped venom onto the mischief-makers face. Saddened by his severe punishment, Sigyn (Loki's wife) volunteered to stay by her husband's side and tend to his needs. She held a bowl to catch the venom of the snake. But when the bowl filled with venom, Sigyn had to leave Loki's side to throw the venom out of the cave.

During this time, the drops that fell onto Loki's face would cause him to violently shake. With such agonizing pain his shaking would tremble earthquakes all the way down to Midgard. This is the fate of Loki and Sigyn until the coming of Ragnarok where

Loki will be freed from the chains and help the giants destroy Asgard.

Ragnarok

While the Norse gods and goddesses could live far longer than humans, they are not immortal. It is evident from the story of Baldur's Death that the Aesir and the Vanir deities can die.

According to the Norse prophecy, the cosmos (along the gods and goddesses) are fated to end. The first of these prophecies are said to have already happened (the birth of Fenrir, Jormungand, and Hel; the death of Baldur, and the punishment of Loki). The gods knew they had to face their fate and that their time will eventually end.

However, they don't despair because of such destiny. They in fact prepare for this tragic fate. Odin built Valhalla, where he houses the strongest, bravest, and most heroic warriors so they can aid him in battle during Ragnarok. But deep down, Odin knew that he indeed would be eventually overthrown.

Upon the coming of Ragnarok, Loki and his son Fenrir would be freed from their chains and begin destroying the Nine Realms. This devastation would cause the Yggdrasil to tremble. A large horde of jotuns would strorm the gates of Asgard led by the returning of Loki. Heimdall is tasked to sound his Gjallarhorn to warn the Asgardians of any incoming attack.

The jotuns would certainly destroy Asgard with so much fury in their possession. Fenrir is forecasted to kill both Odin and Tyr. Not before many warriors in Ragnarok would fight valiantly and die beside them. Thor and his arch-enemy Jormungand will kill each other in a bloody duel. Meanwhile, Loki and Heimdall will also slay one another.

Once Ragnarok ends, the cosmos would then start to heal. The damaged land would sink back into the sea. The realms would be silent and calm until the cycle of life begins again. In the end, Baldur would be resurrected, and a new human pair named Lif and Lifthrasir would be born to repopulate Midgard alongside the remaining living gods. Although many of the gods and jotuns are no more so be the evil that surrounded them.

CONCLUSION

Before the tide of Christianity cast its influence over the greater part of the Western World, magic and tradition were rich in the lives of the Nordic people. These great men and women of lore speak to us of glorified battles, strong noble bloodlines, and honor in the face of adversity. We celebrate the incredible tales of Loki and Frigga, the mighty Thor and the all-powerful Odin. Now the annals of history have offered us the great gift of studying and understanding this magnificent culture.

Readers young and old alike have the opportunity to explore this fascinating and awe-inspiring collection of religious stories and rich traditions belonging to such a complex belief system. Discover for yourself the magic and mystery in the stories of Baldur, Heimdall, and Idun. Uncover the ancient tale of the fortification of Asgard, the great kingdom of the Nordic gods, and the chilling story behind the binding of Fenrir.

Even though thousands of years have passed since these cultural stories were first shared around the forges and fires of the Nordic populations, they still entrance and inspire us with the great deeds of the human race and the incredible gods who watched over them. Find your own wealth of inspiration among the tales of the great gods and goddesses once worshipped by the Vikings.

64

www.ingramcontent.com/pod-product-compliance
Lightning Source LLC
Chambersburg PA
CBHW070316190726
48291CB00013B/1733